THE MOON LADY

AMY TAN

THE
MOON LADY

illustrated by GRETCHEN SCHIELDS

Aladdin Paperbacks

New York   London   Toronto   Sydney   Singapore

First Aladdin Paperbacks edition, November 1995

Aladdin Paperbacks

An imprint of Simon & Schuster, Children's Publishing Division
1230 Avenue of the Americas, New York, NY 10020

Manufactured in China
16 18 20 19 17 15
0820 SCP
The text of this book is set in 15pt. Bembo. The illustrations are rendered in watercolor.

Library of Congress Cataloging-in-Publication Data
Tan, Amy. The Moon Lady / by Amy Tan ; illustrations by Gretchen Schields. —
1st ed.   p.   cm. Summary: Nai-nai tells her granddaughters the story of her outing, as a
seven-year-old girl in China, to see the Moon Lady and be granted a secret wish. ISBN
978-0-689-80616-2 [1. China—Fiction.   2. Wishes—Fiction.   3. Grandmothers—Fiction.]   I. Schields,
Gretchen, ill.   II. Title.
PZ7.T1612Mo   1992   [E]—dc20   91-22321

hree sisters looked out the window of their grandmother's apartment. Dark clouds floated high above. Hard beads of rain danced on umbrellas below. There was nothing to do!

"I wish it would stop raining," said Maggie with a sigh. She was the oldest. It was very hard for her to sit still.

"I wish we could get wet," said Lily, watching a boy ride his bicycle through rain puddles.

June, the youngest sister, huffed on the windowpane, then drew a face on the fog cloud she had made. "Nai-nai," she said to her grandmother. "I wish we had something to do."

"So many wishes on a rainy afternoon," Nai-nai said. And when she saw her granddaughters' faces, she drew them close to her. "I know how it is to wish that the weather were warmer or cooler, sunnier or shadier. I was once a young girl. And I can remember a time when I ran and shouted, too, when I could not stand still."

"You shouted?" asked Maggie with big eyes.

Nai-nai laughed. "You think I don't know how to shout? Oh yes, I shouted very loud. It was the day I told the Moon Lady my secret wish."

"Who is the Moon Lady?" asked Lily.

"What is a secret wish?" asked June.

"So many questions!" Nai-nai said. "Well, sit down and I will tell you—in a story that comes from my childhood in China. It is my earliest memory."

Many years ago, the year I turned seven, the Moon Festival arrived during an autumn that was terribly hot. When I awoke on that morning, the fifteenth day of the eighth moon, the straw mat covering my bed was already sticky. The sun drove rays through the bamboo curtains like knives. And soon the heat was seeping into my pillow, itching the back of my neck, and cooking up the stinky smells of my chamber pot, so that I awoke restless—and full of complaints.

"Amah!" I cried. "It's too hot!" My nursemaid slept on a cot in the same room I did. She lifted me out of bed. But that day, instead of dressing me in the light cotton jacket and loose trousers I usually wore, Amah brought out something heavier. "Too hot!" I complained as Amah slipped the new jacket over my cotton undergarments.

"No arguing," said Amah. "Your mother made you special clothes for the Moon Festival." The jacket and trousers were made out of yellow silk, with black borders and embroidered flowers at the sleeves and ankles. Yellow and black: the colors of a tiger. For that's what I was—a girl born in the year of the tiger, a tiger with a light side and a dark side, a fierce temper and running feet.

I asked Amah if I could wear the tiger slippers my older brother had already outgrown. "If you behave," she answered. She was weaving silk threads into my hair, winding everything into two tight knots, one on each side of my head. Suddenly I heard voices in the courtyard and pretended to tumble off the stool so I could see out the window.

"Ying-ying, stand still!" Amah scolded and pulled me back before I could see anything.

"Who's here?" I asked.

"*Da jya*"—the whole family—said Amah. "Your father has rented a big boat. This afternoon we will all go to Tai Lake. And tonight you will see the Moon Lady . . . if you behave."

"The Moon Lady! The Moon Lady!" I said, jumping up and down. And then I tugged Amah's sleeve and asked, "Who is the Moon Lady?"

"Lady Chang-o," Amah answered. "She lives on the moon. Tonight is the only time you can see her and have a secret wish fulfilled." I imagined a lady dressed in shadows, sitting on the moon, leaning over to find me.

"What is a secret wish?" I asked.

Amah told me, "It is what you want but cannot ask."

"Why can't I ask?"

And Amah had to think hard how to answer me. "If you ask, then it is no longer a wish but a selfish desire," she said at last.

"Then how will the Moon Lady know my wish?" I said.

Amah laughed. "You can ask her because she is not an ordinary person."

"Good," I said. "Then I will tell her I don't want to wear these clothes anymore."

"Ah! Did I not just explain?" said Amah. "Now that you have told me this, it is no longer a secret wish."

That morning nobody seemed in a hurry to go to the lake except me. Mama and the old ladies drank more and more tea. They talked about aches and pains, about herbs and ointments for soothing swollen feet. My father and my uncles recited poetry,

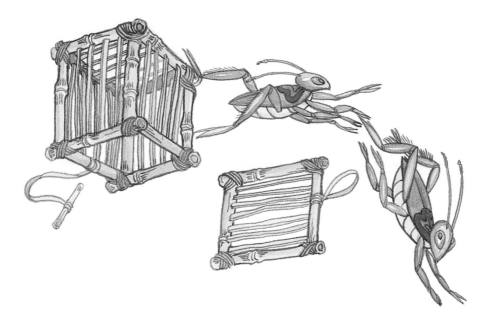

looked at paintings on the walls, listened to a cricket singing in its cage.

I sighed and sighed, impatient to go to the lake, but nobody seemed to notice me. Finally Amah came into the room and gave me a moon cake in the shape of a rabbit. She said I could go into the courtyard and eat the moon cake with my two cousins, Little Mei and Littlest Mei.

It is easy to forget about a boat when you have a rabbit moon cake in your hand. The three of us ran through the round moon gate leading to the courtyard. We scrambled and shrieked to see who would get to the bench first. Since I was the oldest, I sat in the shady part, where the stone slab was cool. My little cousins sat in the sun, staring at me, then at my moon cake rabbit.

Oh, how I wished I didn't have to share! But as soon as I thought that, I knew it was a selfish wish. So I broke off an ear for each of them. Of course, I wasn't being very generous, because the ears were just dough, with no sweet bean paste filling or egg yolk inside. But my cousins were too little to know any better. I ate the

rabbit's round body, rolling my tongue to lick off the sticky sweetness. And after we pinched up every last fallen crumb, my cousins left and I had nothing else to do.

Suddenly I saw a dragonfly with a bright crimson body and transparent wings. I leaped off the bench and ran to chase it, jumping and thrusting my hands upward as it flew away, wishing I could fly.

"Ying-ying!" I heard Amah cry in a scolding voice. She was coming through the moon gate, as were my mother and aunts. "Look at your new clothes!"

My mother walked over to me and smiled. "A boy can run and chase dragonflies, because that is his nature," she explained in a gentle voice. "But a girl should stand still. If you are still for a very long time, a dragonfly will no longer see you. Then it will come and hide in the comfort of your shadow." The other ladies clucked in agreement and then they all left me in the middle of the hot courtyard.

Standing perfectly still like that, I discovered my shadow. It had short legs and long arms, two dark coiled braids just like mine. It had the same mind! When I shook my head, it shook its head. We flapped our arms. We raised one leg. I turned to walk away and it followed me. I ran and it chased me. I dashed into the shade and it disappeared! I shrieked with delight at my shadow's own cleverness. How I loved my shadow, this dark side of me that loved all the things no one else could see.

And then I heard Amah calling, "Ying-ying! It is time to go to the lake!" My shadow and I went running toward her.

Our entire family was standing by the front gate chatting happily, waiting for the rickshaws to arrive. Baba wore a new brown gown. Mama had on a jacket and skirt with colors that were the reverse of mine: black silk with yellow bands. And my older brother had put on a blue jacket fastened with a silver lock on a chain to protect him from ghosts who stole young boys.

When we arrived at the lake I was disappointed to feel no cooling breezes. I jumped out of the rickshaw right away. But then I had to wait many minutes as everyone else slowly climbed out of theirs—Mama, Baba, my uncles and aunts, my brother and cousins.

The lakefront was crowded that day, full of excited people. From where I stood I could already see the large boat our family had rented. It looked like a floating teahouse, with red columns and a slanted tile roof.

And then—finally!—Amah grabbed my hand tightly and helped me walk across the plank onto the boat. As soon as my feet

touched the deck I sprang free. My cousins and I pushed our way past people's legs, past billows of dark and bright silk clothes, eager to explore the entire boat.

I loved the unsteady feeling of almost falling one way, then the other. Red lanterns hanging from the roof swayed with us. We brushed our fingertips along the railings, then ran past the tables in the indoor teahouse. We pushed a swinging door that took us into what looked like a kitchen. A man holding a big cleaver turned and saw us, and we ran back to the front of the boat, scared.

When we returned we found not just familiar faces but a feast! The servants were emptying hampers of food for our noonday meal. And soon bowls and chopsticks and cups appeared. They brought out sacks of apples, pears, and pomegranates, sweaty earthen jars of preserved meats and vegetables, plates loaded with dancing shrimp and freshwater crabs, and stacks of red boxes with four moon cakes each. Enough for everybody—more than I could have wished!

Soon the meal was over. Baba and my uncles burped loudly. Mama and my aunts drifted into the same drowsy gossip over tea. The servants put down our straw mats, and Amah was telling me to be still, to lie down on my mat. And then the whole boat became quiet as everyone napped through the hottest part of the day.

When I was sure everyone was asleep I got up as quietly as a tiger, careful not wake Amah. First I walked to the rail and looked at the lake. It was crowded with boats: rowboats, pedal boats, sailboats, fishing boats, small boats with only an oil-coated umbrella for a roof, and big floating teahouses just like ours.

Then I wandered along the boat. I sneaked past the kitchen where I had seen the scary man with the cleaver, and was suddenly somewhere I had never been. At the back of the boat a man was feeding skinny sticks of wood into a small chimney-pot stove. A toothless woman was chopping vegetables. And two rough-looking boys were squatting by the boat's edge. The bigger boy removed a large, squawking long-necked bird from a bamboo cage. The smaller boy dove into the water and swam to a raft made of hollow reeds. Then the bigger boy threw the bird over the side. It swooped with a flurry of wings, then landed on the surface of the shiny water below.

I walked to the boat's edge just in time to see the bird dive under the water and disappear. In a few seconds, the bird popped back up and in its long beak was a fish still struggling to get away. Before the bird could swallow its catch, the boy on the raft grabbed the fish out of its beak, then threw it up to the boy on the boat, who tossed it into a wooden pail. They did this over and over, and each time I clapped my hands. How I wished I could be one of those boys!

And then I turned around and discovered more interesting things. The toothless woman was now dipping her hands into a bucket filled with eels. I came closer and saw that they looked like black snakes. The woman picked up a long, wiggly one, and with

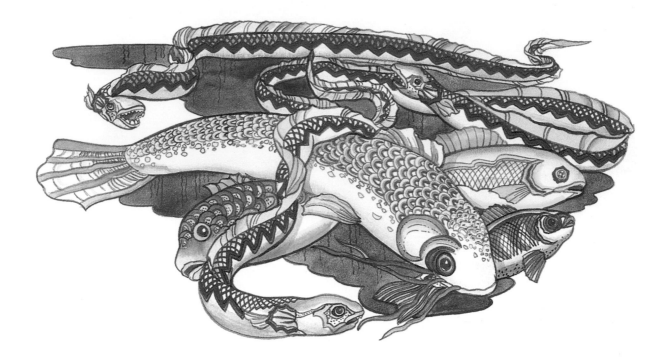

a sharp, thin knife, sliced it from end to end and threw it back into the bucket. I came even closer. The water had turned red. The old woman laughed and said, "tasty soup for your dinner tonight!"

And then her hands became busy again. *Whish! Whish! Whish! Whuck! Whuck! Whuck!* Fish scales flew into the air like shards of glass. Ducks squawked and their feathers floated in front of my eyes like clouds. Buckets of water were thrown on the deck to wash the fishy smells away. Finally, the woman was done. She stood up on creaky legs, carried some baskets of vegetables into the kitchen, and left me alone.

It was not until then that I noticed my new clothes were covered with spots of eel blood, flecks of fish scales, bits of feather and mud. And then I heard Amah's voice: "Ying-ying, where are you?" What a strange mind I had! I quickly dipped my hands into the bucket of eels. I smeared the mess on my sleeves, on the front of my pants, and the rest of my jacket. This is what I truly thought: I could cover the dirty spots by painting all my clothes crimson red, and if I stood perfectly still no one would notice this change.

That is how Amah found me: covered with eel blood. How she screamed! She ran over to see what pieces of my body were missing, what leaky holes I had sprung. And after she inspected my ears and nose, counted my fingers and toes, she yanked off my jacket and pulled off my pants, scolding me in a trembling voice. "Your mother will be glad to wash her hands of both of us." She was angry, but I also think she was scared. You see, she was responsible for me, and when I got into trouble, Amah got into bigger trouble.

"Your mother will banish us to Kunming," said Amah in a sad voice. And when she said that, I was glad! I had heard that Kunming was a wild place surrounded by a stone forest ruled by laughing monkeys.

"When can we go?" I asked. Amah's mouth dropped open, so shocked to hear me say such a thing. She left me standing in my cotton undergarments, pouting at the back of the boat because I refused to say I was sorry.

Evening came, the sky darkened, and the water turned black. I was still sitting at the back of the boat, watching red lantern lights glowing all over the lake. I heard the sounds of happy people at the front of the boat, eager for the banquet to begin. I wished I could be there.

I looked at the water below my bare feet, and I saw my reflection: my legs, my pouting face, my hand waving one of the dirty tiger slippers. And in the dark shiny water, I saw the full moon rising above my head, a moon so warm and big it looked like the sun. The Moon Lady! I had almost forgotten. I turned around

to find her so I could tell her my secret wish. But right at that moment—*pawk! pwak! pwak!*—firecrackers exploded. I lost my balance, and with my tiger slippers still in my hand fell into the water.

The water was cool and at first I was not frightened. I called for Amah, knowing she always came when I shouted for her. And then I began to choke, and water swam up my nose, into my throat and eyes. "Amah!" I tried to cry again, and I was very angry that she did not come right away. And then I felt a dark shape brush against my leg; I was sure it was a swimming snake!

It wrapped around me and squeezed my body like a sponge, then tossed me high into the air. I fell into a rope net filled with wriggling fish. Water gushed out of my throat and now I was wailing, grabbing for my soggy slipper.

When I could finally open my eyes, I saw a large shadow. Another shadow was climbing into the boat. It turned out to be a fisherman, dripping wet. "Is it too small? Shall we throw this little fish back?" The man laughed out loud. Even though it was warm at night, I began to shiver, too scared to cry.

"Stop now," said the other shadow, a woman. "You've frightened her." She turned to me and said in a gentle voice, "Don't be afraid. Are you from another fishing boat? Which one? Point."

I looked out on the lake. My heart was beating fast. I wanted so much to find my family. But instead I saw rowboats and pedal boats, sailboats, and fishing boats like the one I was in, with a long bow and a small house in the middle.

And then—at last!—I saw it. "There," I said, and pointed to a floating teahouse filled with laughing people and swaying lanterns. "There! There!" And I began to cry, now impatient to reach my family. The fishing boat glided swiftly over to the teahouse boat.

"Hey!" the fisherman called up to the boat. "Have you lost a little girl, a girl who fell into the water?"

I heard some shouts from the floating teahouse. I strained to see the faces of Mama, Baba, Amah. People crowded to one side to look at us. They were leaning over, pointing at our boat, laughing with red faces and loud voices.

A little girl pushed her way through some legs. "That's not me!" she cried. "I'm here. I didn't fall in the water." The people on the boat roared with more laughter, then turned away.

"Little miss," said the fisherwoman sadly as we glided away, "you were mistaken." I began to shiver again. I had seen no one who cared that I was missing. The farther we glided, the bigger the world became. And now I felt I was lost forever.

The fisherwoman stared at me. My braids were falling down. My undergarments were wet and dirty.

"What shall we do?" she asked. "No one to claim her."

"Maybe she is a beggar girl," said the man. "Look at her clothes. She is one of those children who ride the flimsy rafts to beg for money."

I was filled with terror. Maybe this was true: I had turned into a poor beggar girl, lost without my family.

"Anh! Don't you have eyes?" the woman said crossly. "Look at her skin, too pale. And her feet, the bottoms are soft. This is the kind of girl who's worn shoes all her life."

I was so happy to hear this! And then I remembered the soggy slipper in my hand. I showed it to the man and woman.

"Ai-ya!" said the woman, staring at the yellow-and-black lump in her hand. "You're somebody's lost treasure, that's for certain."

"Put her on the shore then," said the man. "If she truly has a family that wants her back, that's where they will look for her."

When we reached the dock, the man lifted me out of the boat.

"Be careful next time," the woman called.

On the dock, with the bright moon behind me, I once again saw my shadow. It was shorter this time, shrunken and wild-looking. We ran together over to some bushes along a walkway and hid. I could hear frogs and crickets. And then—flutes and tinkling cymbals, a gong and drums!

From the bushes, I could see a crowd of people, and above them a stage holding up the moon. And then a man burst onto the stage and told the crowd: "And now the Moon Lady will perform a shadow play and sing her sad song to you."

The Moon Lady! And then I saw the shadow of a woman against the bright moon on the stage. She was combing her long hair, singing: "How sad is my fate—to live on the moon, while my husband lives on the sun. Each day and night we pass each other, never seeing one another, except tonight, the night of the mid-autumn moon."

She plucked her lute and sang more: "My husband the master archer shot down ten suns in the eastern sky. He saved the world and received a magic peach for his reward, the peach of everlasting life!"

The shadow of the Moon Lady rose up and opened a box. "When my husband was away," she sang, "I found his magic peach. And wishing I could live forever, I ate it in one swallow."

The Moon Lady began to rise, then fly like a dragonfly with broken wings. "He banished me from this earth, and sent me to live on the moon."

Wyah! Wyah! The sad lute music began again. And now I saw the poor lady standing against the bright moon. Her hair was so long it swept the floor, wiping up her tears. An eternity had passed, for this was her fate: to stay lost on the moon, forever regretting her own selfish wishes.

"For woman is yin," she cried sadly. "The darkness within,

where passions lie. And man is yang, bright truth lighting our minds." The stage went black.

At the end of her tale I was crying with the Moon Lady. I knew her feelings. In one quick moment we had both become lost to the world, and neither of us could find our way back.

Just then, the same young man came onto the stage and announced, "Attention! Attention! And now to thank you for coming, the Moon Lady has agreed to grant one secret wish to each person here." The crowd murmured with excitement. "For a small donation, of course," he added, and everyone booed, and began to walk away. Nobody was listening except my shadow and me.

"I have a wish!" I shouted and ran forward, waving my slipper. But the young man paid no attention to me. So I darted fast as a lizard behind the stage, to the other side of the moon.

And there I saw her—the Moon Lady, glowing with the light from a dozen lamps. She shook her long shadowy hair.

"I have a wish," I whispered, but she did not hear me. And I was thinking fast, remembering all my wishes from the entire day—to take off my hot clothes, to eat a rabbit moon cake by myself, to fly like a dragonfly, to be a carefree boy on a raft.

"I have a wish," I said again, this time a little louder. I walked closer to the Moon Lady. And I could see her face: the shrunken cheeks, a broad oily nose, large glaring teeth, and red-stained eyes. And then her silk gown slipped off her shoulders as she wearily pulled off her long hair. Before the secret wish could fall from my lips, the Moon Lady looked at me and became a man.

Ai-ya! When I saw who the Moon Lady really was, I ran. I ran past the stage and between the bushes. I ran down the pathway, dashing between people walking along the lakefront. I ran up a footbridge. And with the full moon over my back, I shouted what I knew was a true wish from my heart: I wished to be found!

"And now you see," said Nai-nai to her laughing granddaughters, "I did get my wish. Because I am here today to tell you this story. I found them—Mama, Baba, my uncles and aunts, and Amah—waving to me with my other tiger slipper. And when I flew into their arms they cried, 'We found you! At last we found you!' "

Maggie, Lily, and June clapped their hands.

"Of course, I let them think that," said Nai-nai. "But you see, I had already found myself. I found out what kind of tiger I really was. Because I now knew there were many kinds of wishes, some that came from my stomach, some that were selfish, some that came from my heart. And I knew what the best wishes were: those I could make come true by myself."

"Can you think of a wish like that?" Nai-nai asked.

Maggie, Lily, and June looked at each other and smiled. They put their heads together and whispered among themselves, then told Nai-nai their secret wish.

"Oh, what a good wish!" Nai-nai said. "A wish that becomes everyone's wish."

And together Maggie, Lily, and June took their grandmother outside to make their wish come true: They danced with their shadows, shouting, and laughing by the light of the full moon.